Zhu Zhu Pets™

MR. SQUIGGLES' HALLOWEEN PARTY

D1540460

ISBN 978-0-545-26230-9

© 2009 Cepia LLC. Zhu Zhu Pets™ logos, names and related indicia are trademarks of and copyrighted by Cepia LLC. All rights reserved.

Published by Scholastic Inc. SCHOLASTIC and associated logos are trademarks and/or registered trademarks of Scholastic Inc.

12 11 10 9 8 7 6 5 4 3 2 1   10 11 12 13 14/0

Printed in the U.S.A.   40

First printing, July 2010

SCHOLASTIC INC.

New York   Toronto   London   Auckland
Sydney   Mexico City   New Delhi   Hong Kong

Mr. Squiggles loves Halloween. It's one of his favorite holidays! To celebrate, he decided to have a costume party. He invited all of his friends. There would even be a special costume contest.

Nugget wanted a costume that was **DREAMY** and **SWEET**—just like her!

She thought about being a **WISPY CLOUD**, a **RAINBOW**, or...

Nugget the BEAUTIFUL BUTTERFLY!

Num Nums thought about dressing up as
SOMETHING SWEET!

Should she be a **JELLY BEAN,**
a **CARROT,** or. . .

Num Nums the FANCY FAIRY!

Jilly knew she wanted a costume that was **SWEET,** **CHEERFUL,** and **PEPPY**—just like her!

She could be a **PUPPY,** a **BUTTERFLY,** or . . .

Winkie was in **NO HURRY** to pick a costume.

So he decided to dress as a slow-moving critter like himself . . .

Scoodles decided his costume should be
ADVENTUROUS and CURIOUS!

He thought about dressing as a PIRATE, a SPY, or. . .

Scoodles the PILOT!

Pipsqueak wanted a costume that would GO, GO, GO!

So she dressed up as . . .

Patches wanted to choose a costume that showed her LOVE of GARDENING.

She could be a SUN, a ROSE, a TULIP, or...

Rocky loves lots of things: COMIC BOOKS, SUPER HAM, RECYCLING...

...but only one costume suits him!

Chunk thought his costume should be one of his favorite ocean friends: **A FISH** or a **SEA HORSE.**

But he spent all day at the beach so he came to the party as . . .

Mr. Squiggles wanted to dress up as something COURAGEOUS!

He could be a **FIREFIGHTER**, a **POLICEMAN**, or . . .

After he made his costume, Mr. Squiggles decorated for the party. He hung streamers and balloons and set out delicious snacks. He finished just as his guests arrived.

All of the Zhu Zhu Pets were excited
to show off their hard work.